# LOOK AND FIND®

# WOLVERINE AND THE X-MEN™

www.marvel.com

Written by Melanie Zanoza Bartelme
Illustrated by Art Mawhinney

Published by Louis Weber, C.E.O., Publications International, Ltd.
7373 North Cicero Avenue, Lincolnwood, Illinois 60712
Ground Floor, 59 Gloucester Place, London W1U 8JJ

Customer Service: 1-800-595-8484 or customer_service@pilbooks.com

www.pilbooks.com

p i kids is a registered trademark of Publications International, Ltd.

Look and Find is a registered trademark of Publications International, Ltd.,
in the United States and in Canada.

8 7 6 5 4 3 2 1

Manufactured in China.

ISBN-10: 1-4127-3592-0
ISBN-13: 978-1-4127-3592-6

publications international, ltd.

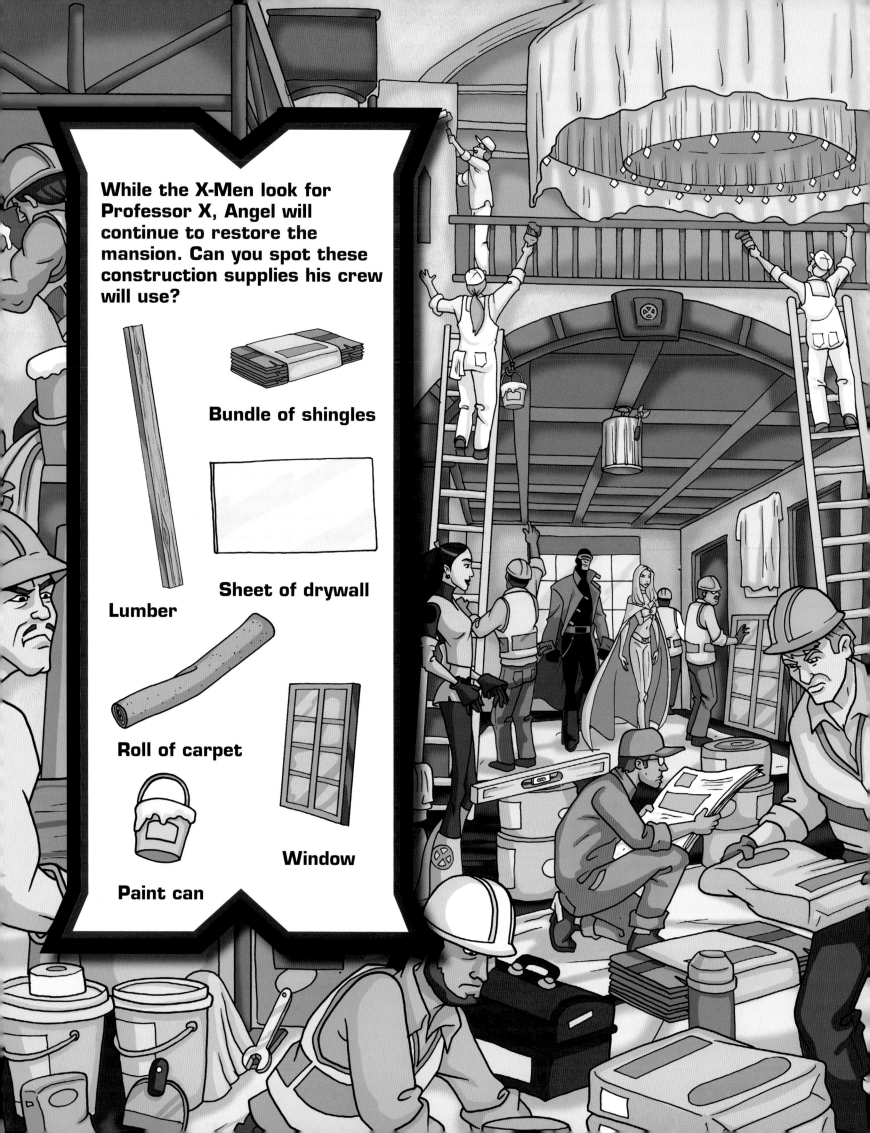

While the X-Men look for Professor X, Angel will continue to restore the mansion. Can you spot these construction supplies his crew will use?

Bundle of shingles

Lumber

Sheet of drywall

Roll of carpet

Window

Paint can

After the great disaster that destroyed his mutant academy, Professor X went missing and the X-Men disbanded. One year later, it's up to Wolverine to reunite the remaining X-Men to find their mentor. Where can he be? And can the X-Men learn to be a team again?

The X-Men are practicing fighting against evil mutants that they might encounter along the way to rescuing Professor X. Do you see these villains in the Danger Room?

**Sabretooth**

**Silver Samurai**

**Toad**

**Magneto**

**Juggernaut**

**Gambit**

**Mystique**

The X-Men traveled to the MRD Detention Center, hoping to find Professor X. Instead they found some other locked-up mutants. While Wolverine and the X-Men help the prisoners escape, look for these guards doing their best to stop them.

The X-Men heard Professor X might be in a village in Africa. The team had no luck finding their leader, but they did come across a teammate: Storm! The people here think Storm is a rain goddess. Can you find these gifts the villagers have offered to her?

This drum

This beaded necklace

This basket of food

This bag

This colorful bowl

This jug

This fabric

The X-Men decided to pay the Brotherhood of Mutants a little visit to see what they knew about Professor X's whereabouts. The Brotherhood didn't give them any info, but the X-Men found something valuable here anyway: Rogue. Look around the hideout for some of the Brotherhood's valuables.

Domino's rifle

Senator Kelly's itinerary

Keys to the stolen jeep

Blob's dumbbells

Rogue's jacket

Communication console

Avalanche's seismometer

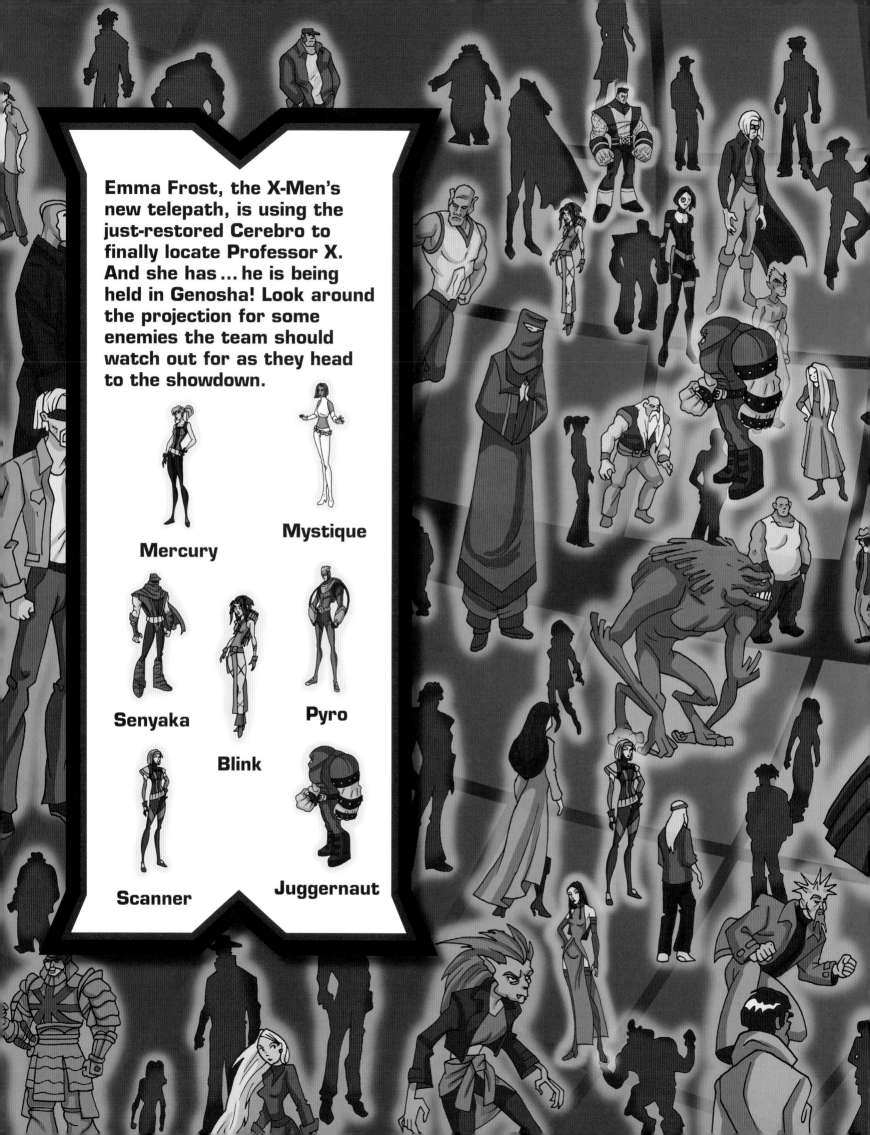

Emma Frost, the X-Men's new telepath, is using the just-restored Cerebro to finally locate Professor X. And she has... he is being held in Genosha! Look around the projection for some enemies the team should watch out for as they head to the showdown.

**Mercury**

**Mystique**

**Senyaka**

**Blink**

**Pyro**

**Scanner**

**Juggernaut**

Wolverine and the X-Men have finally found Professor X! But getting to his cell doesn't look so easy with Magneto's minions standing guard. As the X-Men fight Magneto's forces, look around the battle for these Genoshan residents who'd best get out of the way.

Squidboy

Dust

Network

Shatter

Vindaloo

Fever Pitch

Pixie

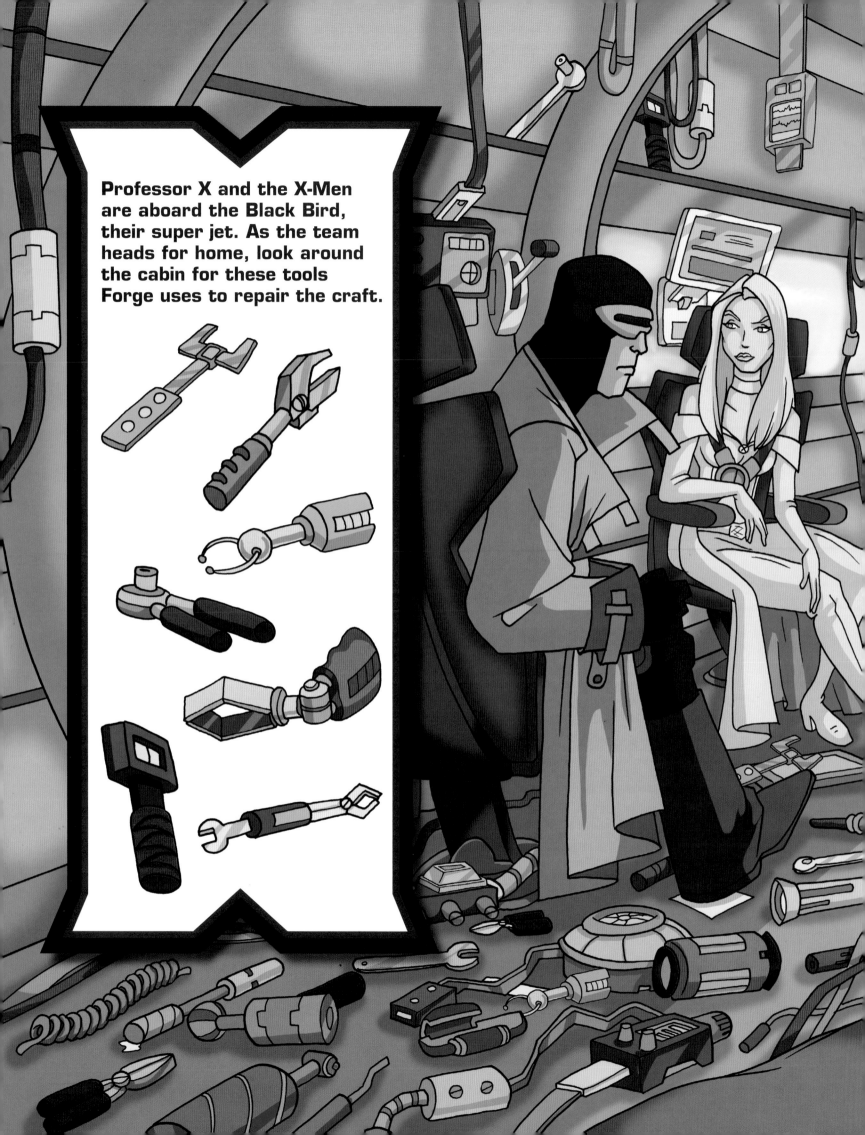

Professor X and the X-Men are aboard the Black Bird, their super jet. As the team heads for home, look around the cabin for these tools Forge uses to repair the craft.

Thanks to Angel, Professor X's mansion is almost rebuilt. Work your way back to the construction site and look for these tools.

Level

Wrench

Hammer

Pliers

Saw

Screwdriver

Pummel your way back to the Danger Room and look for some more bad guys in the simulation.

Spiral

Blob

Mister Sinister

Shadow King

Quicksilver

Pyro

Send yourself back to the MRD Detention Center and look for these escaping mutants.

Boom Boom

Toad

Tilde

Nitro

Rockslide

Dust

Wolfsbane

The evil Shadow King has possessed some of the residents of Storm's village. Can you find them?

Sneak back into the hideout and see if you can spot these stolen items the Brotherhood has stored there.

This box

TV

This crate

Briefcase

Stereo

Jewelry

This laptop

It's good to know where your teammates are. Return to Cerebro and look for these former and future X-Men.

Angel

Jean Grey

Dazzler

Psylocke

Gambit

Colossus

Magneto had a lot of help guarding Professor X. Head back to Genosha and look for some of his minions there.

Pyro

Senyaka

Blink

Mercury

Mystique

Mellencamp

Juggernaut

It takes skill and concentration to maneuver the Black Bird. But the plane wouldn't even get off the ground without all of the buttons and gadgets Forge has installed. Can you spot these?